Time To Get Out

For David McKee

Copyright ©1993 by Fulvio Testa.
This paperback edition first published in 2001 by Andersen Press Ltd.
The rights of Fulvio Testa to be identified as the author and illustrator of this work have
been asserted by him in accordance with the Copyright, Designs and Patents Act, 1988.
First published in Great Britain in 1993 by Andersen Press Ltd., 20 Vauxhall Bridge Road,
London SW1V 2SA. Published in Australia by Random House Australia Pty., 20 Alfred Street,
Milsons Point, Sydney, NSW 2061. All rights reserved.
Colour separated in Switzerland by Photolitho AG, Zurich.
Printed and bound in China.

10 9 8 7 6 5 4 3 2 1

British Library Cataloguing in Publication Data available.

ISBN 0 86264 469 0

This book has been printed on acid-free paper

Time To Get Out

Written and illustrated by

FULVIO TESTA

Andersen Press · London

Slowly a boat sailed across the sea.

Captain Nick was on the look-out, looking for adventure, when an island appeared – a mysterious, tropical island.

He landed the boat and jumped ashore. Straight away he changed into his explorer's costume. He was an explorer, ready for anything.

Then he heard a strange sound. "Zzz, zzz, zzz."
"What is that noise?" he thought, and as he was curious, he set off towards it.

It was Crocodile snoring.
"Why are you snoring so loudly, Crocodile?" asked Captain Nick.
"I'm trying to drown out that other noise," said Crocodile. "It's terrible. Can't you hear it?"

"Knock-knock, knock-knock, knock-knock, knock-knock."
Captain Nick listened and became even more curious. "I'm going to
find out what it is," he said, and left.

It was Monkey smashing coconuts. "What a terrible noise you're making, Monkey!" said Captain Nick.
"I'm trying to drown out that other noise," said Monkey. "It hurts my big ears. Can't you hear it?"

Captain Nick listened. He could hear music being played very badly.
What a din.
"I want to know who's playing!" he said, and quickly set off.

It was the Panthers! They hadn't practised for ages and their music was terrible. It was deafening.

"Why are you playing so loudly?" asked Captain Nick.

"We are trying to drown out that other noise," they said. "It's unbearable. Listen!"

Captain Nick listened. The noise *was* unbearable. It was a strange sound – a rumbling, tumbling, groaning sort of sound, and it was getting louder and louder.

"Let's go and find out what it is," he said, and they all set off.

It was a volcano, a huge, rumbling volcano and as they watched, it started to explode, like a thousand cannons.

What a sight! What a noise!

"Quick," said Captain Nick. "We must escape. It is too dangerous to stay here. I will rescue you from the island and I'll rescue Crocodile and Monkey too."

They all ran through the jungle and reached the boat – only just in time.
They set sail.

They had escaped the volcano and they were in the
middle of the sea.

But the danger was not over. The waves were rising …

Bigger and bigger became the waves. The little boat was barely afloat
until suddenly ...

"SPLASH!" It capsized and they all fell into the water.
"I want to get out of here," said Crocodile.
"I want to get out too," said Monkey.

"Out," said Mum to Captain Nick, "it's time to get out of the bath!"